This book belongs to:

_____

_____

_____

For Noel, Kayleigh, Gem and Holly
and my very special Dad. Thank you.
~ A M

For Paul with thanks!
~ S M

This edition published by Scholastic Inc., 557 Broadway; New York, NY 10012,
by arrangement with Little Tiger Press.
SCHOLASTIC and associated logos are trademarks and/or registered
trademarks of Scholastic Inc.
Scholastic Canada; Markham, Ontario

Original edition published in English by
LITTLE TIGER PRESS,
an imprint of Magi Publications,
London, England, 2005

Text copyright © Ann Meek 2005
Illustrations copyright © Sarah Massini 2005

ISBN 13: 978-1-84506-601-7
ISBN 10: 1-84506-601-4

Printed in China

10 9 8 7 6 5 4 3 2 1

Ann Meek   Sarah Massini

I'm Special,
I'm Me!

Milo looked in the mirror and sighed
a big sigh.

"Come on, Milo, we're going to be late!"
called Mom up the stairs.

Milo pressed his nose right up
against the cool glass.

"What am I going to be today?"
he whispered to himself.

At school, Milo and his friends
were playing a jungle game.
  "Please, can I be the lion?"
asked Milo.
  "No," said Clare. "You're not
strong enough to be king of
the jungle."
  So Milo was a very
sad monkey.

When he got home, Milo peered into
the mirror.

"Who can you see?" asked Mom.

"A monkey," replied Milo quietly.

"Lucky you," said Mom. "How fantastic
to be able to swing through the trees
with all your monkey friends."

"Oh yeah!" said Milo, grinning and
making monkey faces at his mom.

The next day, the children were playing pirates.

"Please, can I be the captain?" asked Milo.

"No," said Ben. "You're too short. The captain has to be tall."

So Milo had to be a deck hand.

"What's wrong?" asked Mom that evening.

"I wish I was tall, like a pirate captain," said Milo.

"I think you are just perfect," said Mom. "Just right for climbing to the top of the sails to be the lookout."

"Wow!" said Milo, smiling. "I never thought of that."

The next day, the children were playing princes and princesses.

"Please, can I be a prince?" asked Milo.

"No," said Jason. "The prince is handsome like me."

So Milo was an unhappy knight.

Later that afternoon, Milo gazed into the mirror.

"Hello there, Milo," said Mom. "Who can you see looking back at you?"

"I can see a knight," said Milo.

"Terrific!" said Mom. "All that shining armor, and you must be brave because only the bravest men are chosen to be knights!"

"Really?" said Milo, a little surprised.

"Definitely," said Mom.

"Cool!" said Milo, pretending to fight a dragon.

The next day, the children were playing spacemen and aliens.

"I'd like to be an astronaut," said Milo, excited.

"No!" said Eloise. "Astronauts can't wear glasses because their helmets won't fit."

So Milo was a little green alien.

Back home Milo gazed at his reflection in the mirror. "Do I look like an alien?" he asked.

"You look just like you," said Mom. "Two eyes, a nose and a mouth, but different from everyone else, and that's what makes you special. That's what makes you my Milo."

Mom put her arms around him. "And anyway, aliens are so lucky to be able to bounce around in space, speaking a secret alien language."

"That's true," Milo smiled. "*Bling, bling, yook, yook,*" he said, bouncing around his bedroom, trying to catch his mom.

The next day, the children
were playing under the sea.
  "I'm going to be a shark," said Alex.
  "I know what I'm going to be!"
said Milo. "I think I'd be a
good stingray, hiding in the
sand, and swimming out
to surprise people. I could
make them JUMP!"
  The children all stared at Milo . . .

"Great idea," said Ben.

"Brilliant!" said Clare.

"Can I be one, too?" asked Alex.

Milo smiled from ear to ear, and ALL the children played stingrays under the sea for the rest of the day.

"That was a great game, Milo," said Ben. "Let's play it again tomorrow."

Milo smiled the brightest smile he had ever smiled.

When he got home that day, Milo
looked carefully into his mirror to
see if he had changed in any way,
but of course he hadn't.

"Mom was right," he said. "I can be
whatever I want to be—I'm ME!"

And in the mirror, Milo's reflection
looked back with a huge, beaming smile!